EPISODE VI
RETURN OF THE JEDI
Read-Along
STORYBOOK AND CD

Hello. I am C-3PO, and you are about to listen to the story of Star Wars: Return of the Jedi.

You can also read along with the story in your book. Unless you are already programmed to know when the pages end, you will know it is time to turn the page when you hear this sound. . . .

I believe the storyteller is ready, so let us begin.

A long time ago in a galaxy far, far away. . . .

Printed in the United States of America

First Edition, April 2015   10 9 8 7 6 5 4

Library of Congress Control Number: 2014952881

FAC-008598-15286

ISBN 978-1-4847-0685-5

DISNEY

LUCASFILM

P R E S S

Los Angeles • New York

SUSTAINABLE FORESTRY INITIATIVE   Certified Sourcing
www.sfiprogram.org
SFI-00993
This Label Applies to Text Stock Only

LUKE SKYWALKER HAD RETURNED HOME TO TATOOINE in an attempt to rescue his friend Han Solo from the clutches of the vile gangster Jabba the Hutt. Luke didn't know that the Galactic Empire had secretly begun construction on a new armored space station even more powerful than the dreaded Death Star. When completed, this ultimate weapon would spell certain doom for the small band of rebels struggling to restore freedom to the galaxy.

On board the new battle station, in a docking bay, Imperial troops stood nervously as Darth Vader's shuttle landed. The Dark Lord approached the commander. "I'm here to put you back on schedule."

"I tell you this station will be operational as planned."

"The Emperor does not share your appraisal of the situation."

"But he asks the impossible."

"Then perhaps you can tell him when he arrives."

"The Emperor is coming here? We shall double our efforts."

"I hope so, Commander. The Emperor is not as forgiving as I am."

On the desert planet Tatooine, C-3PO and R2-D2 had found the palace of Jabba the Hutt, where the frozen Han Solo was being held captive. As the droids stood before Jabba, R2 projected a message.

"I am Luke Skywalker, Jedi Knight and friend to Captain Solo. I seek an audience with Your Greatness to bargain for Han Solo's life. With your wisdom, I'm sure that we can work out an arrangement that will enable us to avoid any unpleasant confrontation."

Jabba growled his answer. There would be no bargain.

Moments later, a mysterious bounty hunter, pulling Chewbacca behind him in chains, approached Jabba's throne. Jabba gleefully paid the bounty on the Wookiee, then sent him to the dungeon.

That night, while everyone slept, the bounty hunter returned and went directly to Han's carbonite slab. He pressed a few buttons on its side, and Han was free of the carbonite. The bounty hunter was Leia!

"I've gotta get you out of here."

A curtain parted, and behind it were Jabba and his gang.

Now they were all prisoners. Han and Chewbacca were in the dungeon, and Leia was Jabba's servant. Suddenly, a dark figure appeared before Jabba. "I'm taking Captain Solo and his friends. You can either profit by this or be destroyed." It was Luke!

The gangster slammed his fist on a table, causing a trapdoor to open beneath the young Jedi. He fell into a filthy pit, where a monstrous creature stomped toward him. Luke dodged its attacks and finally crushed it under the heavy cell door. Jabba was furious!

Jabba then sentenced Luke and Han to die in the Pit of Carkoon, the nesting place of the terrifying carnivorous sand monster.

As Luke walked the plank over the pit, R2-D2 threw
his lightsaber to him. The Jedi swung at his captors. Then
Han and Lando battled the forces on their skiff while Luke
rescued Leia. In a matter of moments, Jabba was dead, and
our heroes were taking off in the *Millennium Falcon* to meet
the rest of the Rebel Alliance.

Much later, Luke left the group and went off on his own to Dagobah. "I have a promise to keep—to an old friend."

When Luke arrived, he found that Yoda was very ill.

"No more training do you require. Already know that which you need. You must confront Vader. Then, only then, a Jedi will you be."

"Master Yoda . . . is Darth Vader my father?"

"Your father he is. Luke . . . there is . . . another . . . Sky . . . walker." The old Jedi Master closed his eyes and vanished.

As Luke prepared to leave, Ben Kenobi appeared.

"Obi-Wan! You told me Vader betrayed and murdered my father."

"Your father was seduced by the dark side of the Force. He ceased to be Anakin Skywalker and became Darth Vader."

"Yoda spoke of another."

"The other he spoke of is your twin sister."

"Leia. Leia's my sister."

"Bury your feelings deep down, Luke. They do you credit, but they could be made to serve the Emperor."

Luke returned to the rebel fleet and joined his friends in the main briefing room, where the plan of the attack was being outlined. One of the admirals announced that the Emperor himself was aboard the new Death Star, overseeing the final stages of the construction.

A strike force headed by General Han Solo would go to the moon of Endor to deactivate the energy shield that surrounded the battle station. At the same time, a group led by General Lando Calrissian would fly into the Death Star to blow up the main reactor.

The strike force landed on the moon of Endor. As they sneaked through its thick forest, they were spotted by a group of stormtroopers on speeder bikes. Luke and Leia jumped onto an available bike and took off. Zooming around the trees, Luke jumped from Leia's bike onto the back of a nearby stormtrooper's and pushed him off.

Suddenly, more stormtroopers raced up behind them. Luke went one way, Leia another. With a swing of his lightsaber, Luke cut the fins of one stormtrooper's bike and it went spinning into a tree.

Luke caught up with Han and found that Leia hadn't returned. They set out to look for her, but were caught in a trap set by the furry Ewoks.

When the Ewoks saw C-3PO, they thought he was a god. They escorted him and the others back to their village, where Leia was waiting. It was there that C-3PO told the Ewoks of our heroes' incredible adventure and their struggle against the Empire. The Ewoks declared our friends honorary members of their tribe and vowed to help in the battle against the Empire.

Seconds later, Leia followed Luke outside. "Luke, what's wrong?"

"Vader is here—now—on this moon. I have to face him."

"Why?"

"He's my father. . . . There's more. The Force is strong in my family. My father has it, I have it, and my sister has it. You are my sister."

Leia looked at her brother. "I know. Somehow I've always known. But why must you confront him?"

"Because there is good in him. I can save him."

Luke left and turned himself over to the Empire, where he was met by Darth Vader. "The Emperor has been expecting you."

"I know, Father."

"So you have accepted the truth."

"I have accepted that you were once Anakin Skywalker, my father."

"That name no longer has any meaning for me."

"Search your feelings, Father. You can't do this. I feel the conflict within you. Let go of your hate."

"It is too late for me, Son."

Lando led his fleet toward the Death Star while Han, Leia, and the Ewoks approached the energy shield on Endor. At the same time, Luke was brought to the Emperor aboard the battle station.

"Welcome, young Skywalker. I've been expecting you. Everything that has transpired has done so according to my design. Your friends on Endor are walking into a trap. As is your rebel fleet."

Luke looked out the window and saw an entire legion of Imperial Star Destroyers waiting for the rebels.

On Endor, the rebels couldn't make a move. Stormtroopers were all over them. "Freeze, you rebel scum."

Suddenly, the stormtroopers were pelted with rocks and sticks as the Ewoks came out of their hiding places and attacked. The battle for Endor had begun.

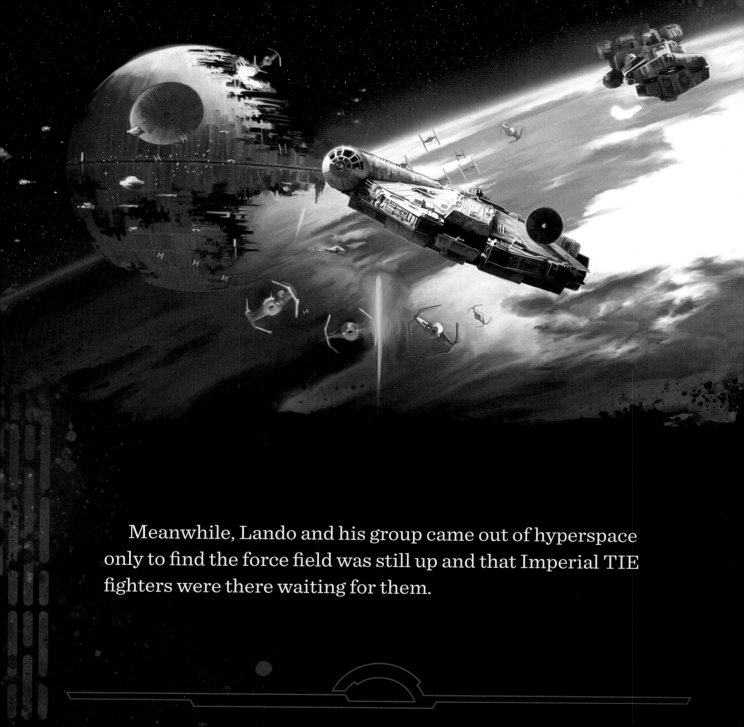

Meanwhile, Lando and his group came out of hyperspace only to find the force field was still up and that Imperial TIE fighters were there waiting for them.

Back aboard the Death Star, the Emperor grinned at the young Jedi. "From here you will witness the destruction of the Alliance, and the end of your insignificant Rebellion."

Luke felt the dark side crawling within him. He controlled it as much as he could, but it was a tough struggle. His lightsaber was within reach. In a flash, it flew to his hand, and he swung at the Emperor. Vader's sword was there, instantly. The Emperor laughed maniacally as Luke's and Vader's swords clashed in a spray of sparks.

On Endor, the Ewoks were gaining ground as the battle wore on. Now there were Imperial scout walkers blasting and smashing their way through the forest. But the Ewoks ambushed the machines by tripping them with vines and crushing them with logs. Meanwhile, Han and Leia were trying to enter the bunker.

High above, Lando was leading an attack on the Imperial Star Destroyers until Han could get the shield down. But time was running out. He couldn't hold the Empire back for too much longer.

Aboard the Death Star, Vader searched for the young Skywalker, who had slipped into the shadows.

"You cannot hide forever, Luke. Give yourself to the dark side. It is the only way to save your friends. Your feelings for them are strong. Especially for—sister! So, you have a twin sister. If you will not turn to the dark side, then perhaps she will."

"No!" Luke went for Darth Vader, slashing wildly. He pounded the Dark Lord with his lightsaber, forcing him to the floor.

The Emperor laughed, and Luke suddenly realized what he had done. He tossed his weapon aside. "I'll never turn to the dark side. You failed, Your Highness. I am a Jedi, like my father before me."

"So be it, Jedi." The Emperor raised his hands. Bright blue bolts of electricity shot from his fingers and zapped Luke. "If you will not be turned, you will be destroyed." More energy struck Luke as he collapsed to the floor. Darth Vader struggled to his feet and stood beside his master.

Meanwhile, the rebels and the Ewoks managed to defeat the Imperial troops. They had placed several bombs in the control room, and in a matter of seconds, the entire shield generator had exploded.

Aboard the *Millennium Falcon*, Lando got word that the shield was down, so he restarted his attack run into the Death Star. Dodging the Imperial TIE fighters, Lando led the rebels through the superstructure and headed straight for the main reactor.

Back in his chamber, the Emperor glared at Luke twisting in pain on the floor. "Now, young Skywalker, you will die." Again, he blasted the Jedi Knight.

Vader looked at his doomed son and then at his master. Suddenly, Vader grabbed the Emperor from the back and lifted him over his head. The Emperor's energy bolts were now blasting Vader as he carried his master over to an open pit. With one final burst of strength, he hurled his evil ruler over the edge. Then the great warrior fell to the floor. Luke crawled to his father's side and pulled him to safety. They were both too weak to move.

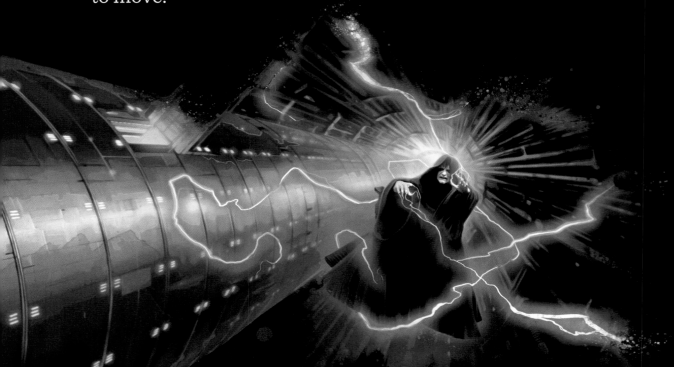

Not far away, Lando and his team found the main reactor and fired at its supports. The massive structure began to collapse. Pursued by flames, the rebels headed for their escape route.

Inside the battle station, Luke dragged his father to the ramp of a shuttlecraft. "Luke, help me take this mask off."

Luke then removed his father's breath screen and looked at the man beneath the mask. "Now go, my son. Leave me."

"No. I can't leave you here. I've got to save you."

"You already have, Luke. You were right about me. Tell your sister . . . you were right." Anakin closed his eyes . . . and was gone.

After Luke pulled his father's armor aboard the shuttle, he lifted off from the docking bay. At that same moment, Lando, chased by flames, flew out of the Death Star. They both managed to escape just as the Death Star exploded in a giant fireball.

Back at the Ewok village, the rebels celebrated their victory over the Empire, while Luke set a torch to his father's armor. As the smoke rose overhead, X-wing fighters flew by, setting off fireworks in the sky. Elsewhere in the galaxy, there were similar celebrations going on.

Off on his own, Luke saw the ghostly images of Yoda, Ben, and his father smiling gratefully. The Jedi smiled back and rejoined his sister and friends.

At last, freedom had been restored to the galaxy.